What's Up, What's Down? Text copyright © 2002 by Lola M. Schaefer Illustrations copyright © 2002 by Barbara Bash
All rights reserved. Manufactured in China by South China Printing Co. Ltd. www.harperchildrens.com

The full-color artwork was prepared with pastels on D'Arches watercolor paper. The text type is Weidemann Black.

Library of Congress Cataloging-in-Publication Data: Schaefer, Lola M., (date) What's up, what's down? / by Lola M. Schaefer ; pictures by Barbara Bash.
p.   cm.   "Greenwillow Books."   ISBN 0-06-029757-3 (trade).   ISBN 0-06-029758-1 (lib. bdg.)   1. Science—Miscellanea—Juvenile literature.
2. Upside-down books—Specimens.   [1. Nature—Miscellanea. 2. Upside-down books.] I. Bash, Barbara, ill. II. Title.
Q173.S287 2002 500—dc21 2001023895

8 9 10 First Edition

What's Up,

What's Down?

BY **Lola M. Schaefer**

PICTURES BY **Barbara Bash**

Greenwillow Books
An Imprint of HarperCollinsPublishers

↑

Follow the arrows
and let your eyes travel up,
reading from the
BOTTOM of the page
to the TOP.

Then, halfway through,
turn the book around and
let your eyes travel down,
reading from TOP
to BOTTOM.

WHAT'S UP
if you're a mole?

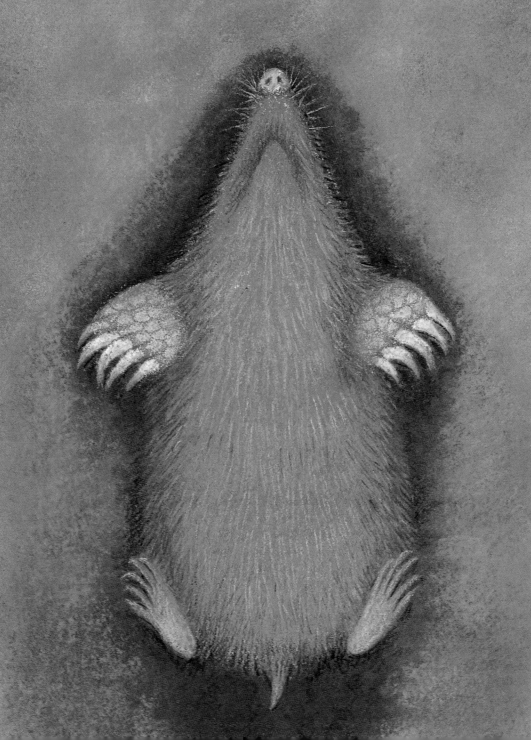

Loose, rich soil
sewn together with
thread-fine roots.

What's up
if you're
a root?

**What's up
if you're the
grass?**

Proud, new grass
pushing emerald
blades toward the sun.

**What's up
if you're a
wildflower?**

A sea of wildflowers
rising and falling
in tides of color.

Whisper-thin
butterfly wings
fluttering above
petal cups.

**What's up
if you're
a butterfly?**

Tall trees
spreading leaves
into umbrellas
of shade.

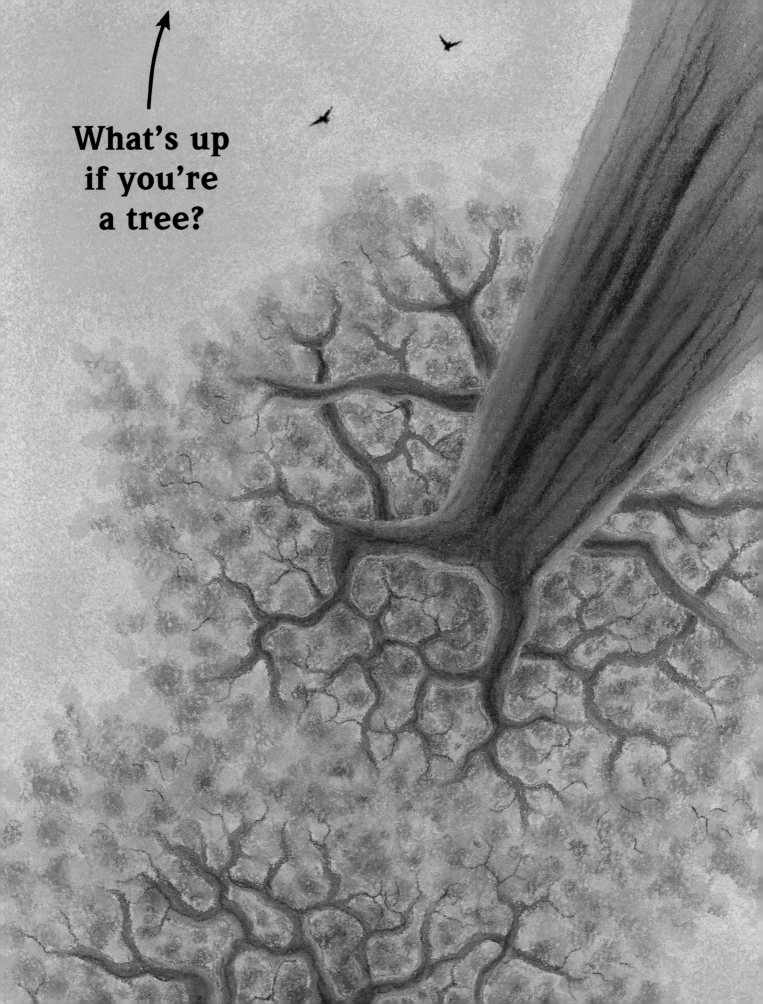

What's up
if you're
a tree?

The traffic of birds
rushing here and there
on invisible highways.

**What's up
if you're
the sky?**

**Bold, blue sky
wrapping the world
in fresh, clear air.**

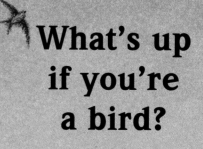

**What's up
if you're
a bird?**

The pearly moon
hanging high,
reflecting soft, glowing
light into space.

WHAT'S DOWN
if you're
the moon?

Feathery, white clouds
swirling over land and sea.

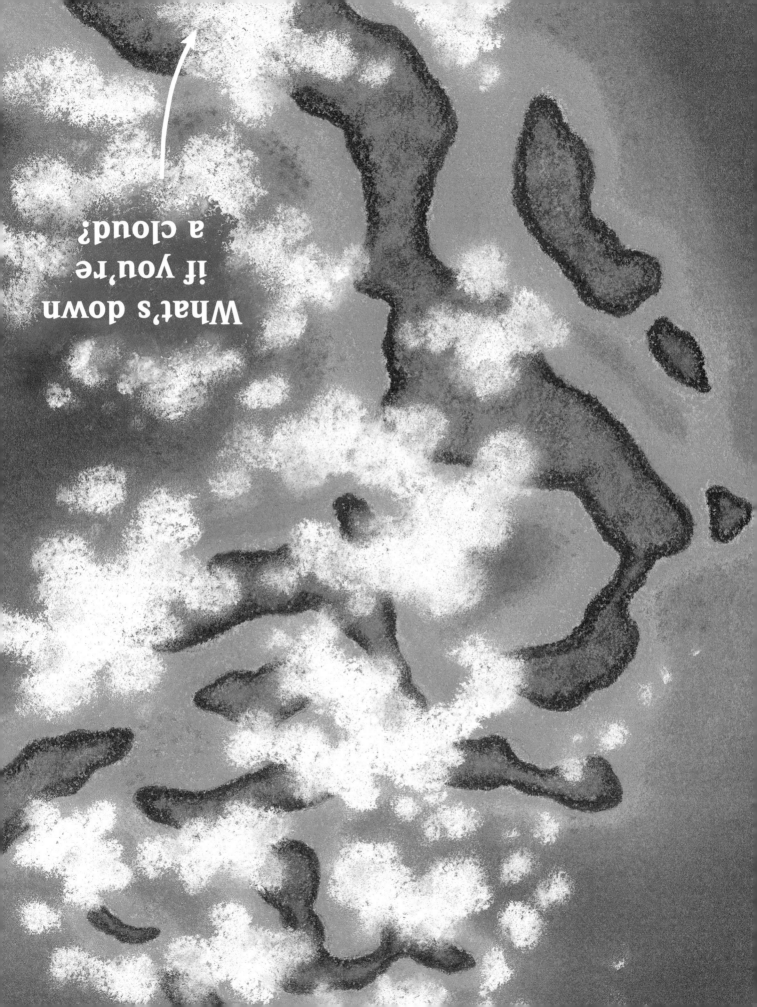

What's down
if you're
a cloud?

Rows of ocean waves,
swelling, surging,
splashing, crashing.

What's down
if you're
a wave?

A playful pod of
whales swimming
to their winter home.

What's down
if you're
a whale?

A ballet of seaweed twisting and twirling in endless currents.

What's down if you're seaweed?

A graceful ray
gliding silently
on wing-like fins.

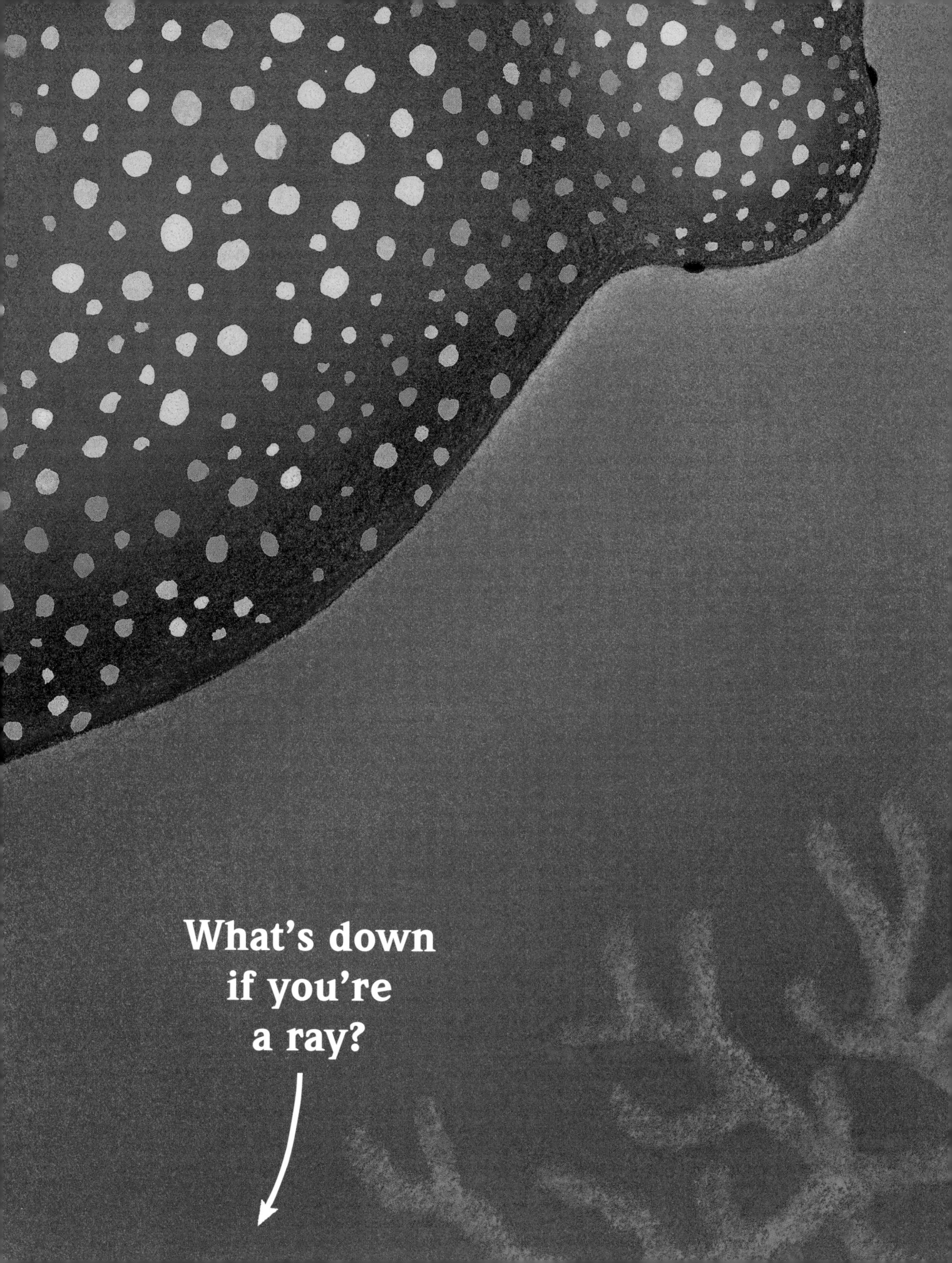

An undersea park of giant sponges hosting creatures, large and small.

What's down if you're a sponge?

A sleek octopus
jetting toward
a hidden cavern.

What's down
if you're
an octopus?

Deep-sea fish
flashing and flickering
in the ink-black waters.

What's down if you're a deep-sea fish?

**Layers of loose mud
blanketing the ridges and canyons
of the rocky crust**

at the
bottom
of the
WORLD.

For Ted—L. M. S.

For Ed, who opened my eyes—B. B.